๏ Mudcat Kids ๏

SLEEP
LITTLE CENTIPEDE
SLEEP

SUSAN E. MERRITT

Illustrated by Andy Cienik

Vanwell Publishing Limited

St. Catharines, Ontario

Design: Linda Moroz
Editor: Angela Dobler

Vanwell Publishing Limited
1 Northrup Crescent
P.O. Box 2131
St. Catharines, Ontario L2R 7S2

Printed in Canada

04 03 02 01 00 99   6 5 4 3 2 1

Canadian Cataloguing in Publication Data

Merritt, Susan E.
    Sleep little centipede sleep

(Mudcat kids)
ISBN 1-55125-021-7

I. Cienik, Andy. II. Title. III. Series

PS8576.E748S53   jC813'.54   C99-930105-5
PZ7.M47S1 1999

ISSN: 1482-7638

To Blake

About the Author

Born and raised in London, Ontario, Susan Merritt received her BA in English and her law degree from the University of Western Ontario. She is the author of the award winning *Her Story* and *Her Story II: Women from Canada's Past*. *The Stone Orchard*, her young adult novel, was shortlisted for the Geoffrey Bilson Award for historical fiction. Her first Mudcat Kids series chapter books, *Cheddar* and *Down in the Dumpster*, are winners of the Canadian Children's Book Centre 'Our Choice' Award. Susan lives in Ridgeway, Ontario with her husband and two children.

CONTENTS

CHAPTER ONE

The Thing

George Cortino jolted awake in the night. Somewhere nearby, a siren whooped and wailed. He could hear his parents stumbling around in their bedroom across the hall.

George's father appeared in the dark doorway with a flashlight and two baseball bats. "No lights," Mr. Cortino hissed as George reached for the lamp. "Someone must have broken in downstairs. They've set off the alarm system in the store."

George's heart began to pound. Burglars!

"C'mon," whispered his dad. "Your mom has already called the police, so you and I are going to go down and check around. With all this noise, the burglars are long gone. But here's a bat, just in case."

"What about me, Dad?" said Harold from his bed on the other side of the room.

"You stay up here with your mom."

"Awwwww."

"She may need your help, Harold. So just do as you're told."

"Awwwwww, I never get to do anything good," Harold whined.

It was just like his little brother to try to tag along, thought George as he pulled on his jeans. What a pest.

George and his dad crept down the back stairs to the store below. Mr. Cortino flipped a switch and the siren dropped to a moan, then faded away. He flipped another switch and the store flooded with light. The place looked the same as usual.

Officer Silva began to pound on the front door and Mr. Cortino quickly let him in.

"Nobody here, officer. And there's no sign of a break in. Guess you came for nothing."

"Well now, that's alright, Juan. You've only had the motion detector in your store for a week or so. Guess it's time for your first false alarm."

The officer walked over to the motion detector.

"Juan, are you sure there's nothing crossing the beam of light?" Officer Silva shrugged, "'Cause even a little thing can break its path and set the siren off. Once I was called to an office building with a couple of big potted trees inside. A leaf had fallen off one of the trees and through the beam of light. That was enough to set off the alarm!" He shook his head in amazement. "One little leaf!"

George stared at the small hole in the wall where the motion detector had been installed. Above the hole was a wooden shelf, empty except for a few cobwebs. When the alarm system was turned on, it looked like a tiny flashlight was sending a band of light across the store. George studied the path the beam of light would travel, but there was nothing blocking its way.

They checked the store one more time. Then Officer Silva said good-bye and returned to his patrol car. The

Cortinos locked up, reset the alarm and returned to bed.

The next morning George's school, J.J. Metcalf, was buzzing with stories.

"Hey George, is it true someone broke into your store and took all the hammers?"

"Hey Cortino, I heard a motorcycle gang came and stole all your money. 'Zat true?"

"Hey George, did a couple of drunks really break into your dad's store? I heard the cops found them asleep beside the coffee machine."

Everyone was disappointed when George told them the siren had been a false alarm.

After first recess, George, who had arrived early for gym class, began to feel drowsy. Jumping out of bed at three in the morning to look for burglars had tired him out.

He felt sleepier and sleepier as he sprawled on the cold, hard gym floor. He rolled over onto his stomach and buried his head in the corner of his arm. He could hear voices down the hallway and knew the rest of his class was coming.

Then he felt a sharp pinch. Surprised, George lifted his head to take a look. A brown, hairy-looking thing about the size of his thumb crouched on his wrist. With a yelp George shook it off. The hairy thing sailed across the room toward the doorway just as Jeannie, Holly and Monica walked into the gym.

It bounced off Jeannie's leg and tumbled to the floor. Holly shrieked and jumped back. The hairy thing paused, then turned and scuttled toward Holly, who gave another ear-piercing shriek.

Jeannie ran forward and squashed it with one quick step.

"Ewwwwww, what was that?" cried Holly.

Jeannie calmly examined the bottom of her running shoe.

"It's a centipede." She shrugged. "I see them all the time in my granny's barn."

Monica came closer. "Look! The legs are still moving...no wait. They've stopped."

Holly made a face. "Creepy. All those hairy legs," she shuddered.

"Yeah, a centipede has at least thirty

legs. They can bite, too," said Jeannie in a matter-of-fact way. Jeannie knew a lot about bugs. She usually did her science projects on them.

George jumped to his feet and studied his arm. There was a puffy red spot, bigger than a quarter, on his wrist. The darn thing had bitten him! He knew spiders could bite, but centipedes...?

"Are they poisonous?" George kept his voice calm. He did not want to make a big deal about a bug bite, but it was really sore!

"Yeah. They kill spiders and insects and stuff like that with their poison bite," Jeannie said calmly. "Then they eat 'em."

She studied the bottom of her shoe and added "But I don't think their bites are poisonous to people. Not the ones around here."

The rest of the class poured into the gym, eager to find out about the screams. They crowded

around Jeannie, and admired the squashed centipede on the bottom of her shoe.

"Cool," said Michael. "My cat eats those things. He catches them in our basement."

Someone else claimed her little brother tried to stick them up his nose.

That made Holly squeal. "Gross. That thing tried to attack me," she said nervously.

Monica pointed at George who was rubbing his wrist. "I think it bit George."

"Was that you screaming, little Georgie?" grinned Ziggy. He gave his glasses a quick push.

"Ha, ha, ha," muttered George. Ziggy Ziggler was always a wise guy.

"George," said Ziggy, suddenly serious, "how do you stop infection from bug bites?"

Infection! George hadn't thought about that. "How?" he asked.

Ziggy snickered. "Don't bite any bugs."

"Very funny, four eyes," muttered George.

Ziggy smiled. "The better to see you with, little Red Riding Hood." He continued in a raspy voice, "Come closer little Georgie. I'm a sweet old centipede and you look good enough to eat!"

George could not think of a reply, so he turned and walked away. But he stopped rubbing the red bump. When you were the biggest kid in class, everyone expected you to be made of steel or something. He couldn't make a big deal about the bite even though he had always hated things with a zillion hairy legs. He didn't mind snakes or big dogs. He didn't mind thunderstorms. He didn't even mind stuff like ants or spiders. But anything with a zillion legs gave him the creeps.

George had carefully kept this fear of his a secret. If Harold ever found out, well, a little brother could make life miserable over a thing like that. So when gym class began, George played indoor soccer with the rest of the kids and said nothing about the bite.

Just before the end of gym, Ms. Hampson, their homeroom teacher, showed up and made an announcement.

"We're going to visit the Junior Kindergarten classroom after lunch recess. You are all becoming reading buddies with the JKs."

Everyone knew she was talking about the little kids in Junior Kindergarten. There was a buzz of excitement.

Ms. Hampson held up her hand for silence. "Now I want you to understand that you will be more to the little JKs than just reading buddies." She looked around at the class.

"They will look up to you as important big kids. I want you to be role models for them. And I want you to always set a good example. Is that understood?"

She looked around at the nodding heads and continued, "Now today I want each of you to take time to get to know your new reading buddy."

George groaned. Reading to a bunch of babies would be a drag, he thought. He gently rubbed the red bump on his wrist. It was still sore and now it was beginning to itch.

This new reading buddy would probably tag around after him, George thought gloomily, just like his little brother. What a pain.

But the rest of the class was excited at the news.

"Hurrah! We'll be missing more school," said Michael. "First gym class and now this. What a great day." He gave Ziggy a playful punch as the class left the gym.

Ziggy grinned. "Four-year-olds say such funny things. It's gonna be a scream."

Monica, who was an only child, smiled. "I love little kids," she said dreamily, "they're sooooooo sweet."

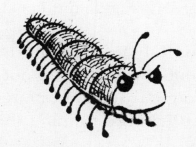

CHAPTER TWO

Skinny Pigs

"George," said Ms. Hampson, "you will be Chad's reading buddy. Come and meet him."

Chad turned out to be a pale, thin boy with a mass of curly brown hair. He was neatly dressed in pressed jeans and a fancy sweater.

"Wow. Look at the designer clothes on your reading buddy," Monica whispered to George. "He's really cute," she added.

George said nothing but led Chad over to a huge green frog-shaped cushion on the floor.

Chad carefully brushed off the cushion before sitting down. He did not even look at George. Instead, he stared down at his own bright red running shoes.

They were held on with blue Velcro strips instead of laces. Chad picked a bit of dust off one shoe.

George was amazed. He had never seen a kid like this, except maybe Monica, who was the class neat-freak. His little brother Harold was a slob. Then again, so was he. In fact most of the kids he knew were slobs.

Chad held up a picture book called *Trucks, Trucks and More Trucks*, and said "This one!"

George smiled. He remembered his dad reading this book to him when he was little. George opened it up and began to read aloud. "Trucks are our friends."

He turned the page. "Trucks-"

"Tomorrow is Pet Show and Tell Day," announced Chad.

George looked up from the book. "Yeah?"

"It's Jewel Ann's turn." He pointed to a little girl with short blonde curls. She was picking her nose, and Monica, who sat beside her, was telling her to stop. Jewel Ann pulled her finger out of her nose and quickly wiped it on Monica's shoe.

Chad tugged George's sleeve. "My cousin had a pet. It was a pig. A skinny pig. But it went away. Now she's getting another pig. Very, very soon."

"Your cousin must live on a farm, then," said George. He tried to sound interested.

"She lives in New York City."

Now George really was interested. "Can you keep pigs in a city?" he asked. Chad shrugged.

The kid must be mixed up, thought George. Maybe he's talking about a toy, or something. "Uh, just what is a skinny pig?" he asked.

"It's a pig that's skinny," replied Chad.

George sighed and shook his head. He returned to the picture book and began to read aloud. "Trucks come in all sizes."

He pointed to one of the trucks on the page. "Look Chad. They use these big trucks to cut down trees."

"My cousin gave some tree leaves to the skinny pig. It's name was Fluffy." Chad sighed. "Fluffy ate the tree leaves. Then Fluffy was very, very gone."

Chad picked a piece of lint off his sleeve.

"Poor little skinny pig," he said calmly.

A pig named "Fluffy"? Then a light went on in George's head. "Wait a minute. Skinny pig! I bet you mean 'guinea pig'! Was Fluffy a guinea pig?"

"Ginn-ee pig? Maybe." Chad shrugged. "Read some more, Joe."

"My name is George."

"Read some more," demanded Chad.

George didn't like to be ordered around by a four-year-old. "What do you say?" George said sternly. Then he almost choked. He couldn't believe he'd said that. He had sounded just like a grown up.

"Please, Joe."

"It's George."

"Please!"

George returned to the book and tried again. "Trucks are important. They do many things for us. They-"

"Soon it will be my turn to bring a pet."

"Yeah?" George gave up on the book. At least he was getting to know his reading buddy better. The little weirdo.

"What kind of pet?"

"An im-portant pet." Chad studied his

15

shoes. There was a wrinkle in one of the blue Velcro strips and he carefully smoothed it out.

"My pet has lots and lots and lots of legs. He lives in a jar with a hole in the top. Sometimes I sing to him." Chad lowered his voice. "My pet's a secret. But I'll tell you 'cause you're my reading buddy, Joe."

"It's George."

Chad lowered his voice. "My pet's a...," he mumbled something that George could not understand.

"What? I couldn't hear you, Chad."

"My pet is a...," again he mumbled.

What kind of pet would have a lot of legs and live in a jar, George wondered. Some sort of bug, he decided. George looked down at the itchy red bump on his wrist. "A centipede?" he asked doubtfully.

"That's right!" Chad clapped his hands and gave a big smile. "A sen-da-peed." He dragged the word out as if he liked its sound. "A sen-da-peed is important! Sometimes I pick up the jar and sing to it. Like this." He began to sing

softly, "Today's the day the sen-da-peeds have their picnic."

Chad's face became serious. "But it's a secret. Okay?"

A secret with a zillion hairy legs, thought George with a shudder. His weird little buddy had a weird little pet.

"Read some more to me!" Then Chad added, "Please?"

George glanced around the room. Most

17

of the kids were on their second picture book, so it was time to speed up.

"You have to stop talking, Chad. Just listen."

George thought of something and reached into his pocket. "Here. If you keep quiet for the rest of the book, I'll give you this."

He held up a small, plastic gorilla he'd found in the school sandbox.

Chad gave him a huge smile. "Okay Joe. I'll be quiet now."

"My name is ... oh, never mind," said George.

CHAPTER THREE

Any Gorillas in Your Pocket?

Two nights later the burglar alarm went off in Cortino's Hardware just before midnight. Again George and his dad went down into the store. Nothing. Again Officer Silva showed up and checked the store. Nothing.

Mr. Cortino told the officer that he would get the company to fix the alarm system. No more false alarms, he promised.

George had just crawled back into his bed when the siren began to whoop and wail a second time! Again George and his father stumbled down the stairs. Nothing. Officer Silva did not even bother to get out of his patrol car.

"All these alarms! No wonder the darn system was on sale." Mr. Cortino shook his head as they wearily climbed back up to the apartment. "First your heart races at the noise," he said, "But you feel so flat when there's nothing there. You're happy there was no burglar, but still…flat. Almost let down," he shrugged.

George nodded and crawled back into his bed. The bite on his wrist still itched sometimes, and he scratched it as he fell asleep.

He dreamed a centipede was crawling around in his hair. The nightmare was so real that George woke with a start. He frantically shook his head and pawed at his hair until he realized he'd been dreaming. Then he had trouble getting back to sleep.

The next afternoon, Ms. Hampson had a little chat with the class before she sent them to visit their reading buddies. "The JKs think a big, friendly monster lives in the school. Sometimes the monster leaves big footprints around their hallway and they try to catch it."

"That is so cute," murmured Monica.

"Anyway, class," said Ms. Hampson, you are to go along with the monster story because the JKs are loving it. So don't spoil your reading buddies' fun. Is that understood?"

Everyone nodded their heads. As George nodded, he scratched his wrist and looked down at the centipede bite. It was itchy again, and still puffy.

"All right, class," finished Ms. Hampson. "Off you go."

Down in the JK room Chad skipped up to George. The other JKs looked rumpled and grubby, but Chad's shirt and pants were spotlessly clean and pressed.

"Any gorillas in your pocket today, Joe?"

Great, thought George. My reading buddy can remember a dumb plastic toy but he can't remember my name.

"No, Chad, I don't have a gorilla in my pocket." He did have a black plastic ant about the size of his thumb, but he wasn't going to tell Chad that. Someone had given him some cheap plastic bugs one Christmas when he was small. George had always thought they were strange but decided Chad might like them.

They sat down on the frog cushion and George began to read. Chad had chosen *Trains, Trains and More Trains*.

George began to read aloud. "Trains are our friends. Trains come in-"

"Jewel Ann brought her lobster in for Pet Show and Tell. Then her mommy took it home."

"Her lobster? That's a weird pet."

Chad carefully straightened the ridges in his socks. "No. It was nice," he said softly.

The only lobsters George had ever seen, were green. They had been in a tank of water in a fancy seafood restaurant. But when you had a sunburn, everyone said you looked as red as a lobster. So, were lobsters green or red, he wondered? Maybe, he thought, lobsters didn't turn red until they were cooked.

"Was the lobster green or red?" George asked.

"It was brown!" Chad said. He looked up at George as if he were crazy.

George remembered the little brown crayfish he sometimes caught in Crooked Creek just outside Williamsville. Chad must mean crayfish, thought George. Crayfish stayed alive for days when they were kept in water.

"Well, does Jewel Ann keep her pet in a bucket of water or in a fish tank?" George asked.

Chad looked shocked. "You don't put lobsters in water. It's very, very, very bad for them."

George was confused. "Well, where do you put lobsters?"

"You put them in a little cage. Then they run round and round on a little squeaky wheel. Like skinny pigs."

Oooooooh, thought George. The little weirdo had done it again. "You don't meant a lobster, Chad. You mean a *ham*ster. Jewel Ann brought in a pet hamster."

Chad shrugged and began to smooth out the Velcro strips on his shoes. "Can you read some more for me, Joe?"

"My name is George, not Joe."

"Okay. Read some more."

"Trains come in all sizes. Trains are important." George pointed to a picture of a train travelling through mountains.

"The monster is im-portant!" announced Chad.

Oh yeah, the pretend monster, thought George. He remembered what Ms. Hampson had told the class.

"Is that so?" he said, pretending to be interested.

"Yes," said Chad proudly. "I have seen the monster." He dropped his voice and leaned toward George.

"I saw him chasing after Jewel Ann."

"Yeah?" said George.

"Yes," whispered Chad. "The monster thinks she will be good to eat."

"Yeah?" George looked over at Monica's reading buddy. She had a plump, pink face and pale yellow hair.

"Why does she look good to eat?"

"Because the monster likes pizza," Chad said loudly. "And Jewel Ann's hair looks like pizza cheese!"

Chad beamed proudly, "Ask me about

24

the monster. I know allllll about him."

"Well," George pretended to think hard. "Where does the monster live?"

"Outside in the dumpster. I saw him there."

"What does the monster do?"

"He goes out with his mommy. And his wife. They eat pizza."

"What if there's no pizza?"

"He eats people. But afterwards he chews gum so his breath will smell nice."

Hmmm, thought George, that's not what I would call a friendly monster...

He decided it was time to start reading again.

George began, "Some trains are big and some trains are small." George point-ed to the picture of a toy train.

"My pet sen-da-peed is small. One day I'm going to bring him here," said Chad. "He has a new name." He gave George a big smile. "Now I call him Joe, after you."

"My name's not..." He stopped. Better "Joe the Centipede" than "George the Centipede". The kids in his class would laugh themselves sick with that one.

"Yeah?" said George.

"I sing him to sleep every night." Chad pretended to be rocking something in the palm of his hand while he softly sang "Sleep little sen-da-peed, sleep." Then he whispered, "And Joe the Sen-da-peed falls asleep."

Chad began to carefully fold back his shirt cuffs. When he folded them back, he made sure the folds were perfectly straight.

George looked around the room. The others were on their third or fourth picture book.

"Look Chad, we still have more reading to do. You'll have to listen now. No more talking about your pet centipede. Okay?"

Chad shoved the train book away. "I don't want this, Joe." He handed another book to George. A man wearing a raccoon cap was on the cover. "This one," said Chad. "I saw him on TV."

It was *The Adventures of Davy Crockett*, another book that George used to read. "This is a good one, Chad!" said George.

Chad began to sing, "Davy, Davy Crockett. King of the Wild Front Ears."

Quickly Chad leaned over and flicked
the ears of the little boy who sat near
him. The other boy let out a howl.

"Stop it, Chad," said George. He was
trying not to laugh. "It's not 'front ears'.

27

It's 'frontier'. The song goes 'King of the Wild Frontier'."

"What's a 'fron-teer'?" asked Chad.

"Just a place," said George.

"I think fron-teer is an im-portant word," said Chad. "Just like sen-da-peed." He looked up at George, then smiled slyly. "Are you sure you don't have any gorillas in your pocket, Joe?"

"It's George. George Cortino. And no, I don't have any gorillas. But you can have this," he held out the black plastic ant, "if you don't talk 'til I tell you to."

Chad's eyes lit up with joy. "This can be Joe's friend."

"Whatever." George was too tired to argue. He began to read aloud again. "Once there was a man named Davy Crockett."

Chad smiled up at George and patted the plastic ant.

CHAPTER FOUR

Very, Very Gone

The next day, Ms. Hampson took George's class to the school library. "Tiger Talk", the J.J. Metcalf newsletter, had announced it was "Get to Know Your Library Week". The article had been right next to the usual "Head Lice Alert".

The class found the library door decorated with a poster of the school's tiger mascot reading *The Three Little Pigs*. It was hot inside and George began to grow sleepy. When the school librarian began to drone on to the class about the history of libraries, George grew even sleepier. He yawned and, safely hidden at the back of the room, dropped his head down on one of the library tables.

Zora Parks, one of his classmates, poked him with her pencil.

"Desk drool is disgusting, George," she whispered.

"Can't help it," he muttered, without raising his head. "Our burglar alarm went off last night."

"Again?"

"Yeah. It's gone off at least four times since we put it in. This time it went off at five in the morning," George groaned softly. "And I'm tired." He scratched his wrist.

"Did the cops come again?" Zora asked.

"Yeah, but they might not come any-more. Not unless we get it fixed. They're tired of all the false alarms." He yawned again. "So's my family. I wish we'd never had the motion detector put in."

When it came time to research a topic, George decided to look up centipedes. He was wondering about the bite on his wrist. It wasn't red or itchy any more, but still...

All the insect books were in use, so George sat down at the row of library computers and did a search on the Internet. The first web site talked about the "house centipede" which has fifteen pairs of legs. George felt better when he read that their bites were harmless to people.

But the second web site was almost scary. In some parts of the world, it said, centipedes grew almost as long as his arm! These centipedes used their poison fangs to catch and kill their prey. They could eat birds, reptiles and even small mammals. Ugh! The thought of a monster centipede killing and eating a sparrow or a lizard or a chipmunk was just plain creepy, George thought as he left the library.

That afternoon when his class showed up for Reading Buddy time, they found a note printed in large, neat letters, taped to the Junior Kindergarten door.

"Dear Reading Buddies," it read, "We will be back very soon. Right now we are hunting for our friendly monster. Please wait here, or join us for a snack in the gym. Your JK friends."

The rest of the class rushed off to the gym, hoping the snack would be a good one, but George stayed behind. He felt too tired to fight over some dumb snack. And besides, he was sure it would only be something healthy, like carrot sticks.

The room was peaceful and George sprawled across the frog floor pillow, too tired to move. But he looked up when he felt something tickle his little finger. Crouched beside his hand was a hairy-looking brown thing.

George couldn't believe his eyes. Another centipede! He snatched his hand away and the centipede scurried toward his leg. Creepy! George scrambled up from the floor and flattened the cen-tipede with his foot. He checked his hand, but there were no bites.

Just then Jeannie walked in, hand in hand with her reading buddy. "They couldn't find the monster," Jeannie said, "so everyone's coming back."

George stood there, stunned. Had he sud-denly turned into bug bait, he wondered?

"Hey George," Jeannie continued, "I hear it's a big day for your little reading buddy."

"Yeah?" George put the thought of an

enormous centipede attacking and eating a
chipmunk firmly out of his mind. "Is it
Chad's birthday or something?"

"No. Chad told me that it's his turn to show his pet to the class. He says its name is 'Joe'. But he wouldn't tell me what it is. He says it's a secret. Maybe it's a pretend pet."

Jeannie's reading buddy, a little boy who always had a runny nose, said excitedly, "No it's a for real pet. Chad brought it in a jar!"

Today? George remembered the centipede he had just killed and began to feel uneasy.

He tried to sound casual. "Uh, did Chad show you his pet?"

Jeannie was shaking her head when her reading buddy pounced on something on the floor. "Here it is," he said, holding up a clear plastic peanut butter jar. "See!" Then he picked up something else and waved it in the air. "Here's the lid."

George and Jeannie peered at the jar. It was empty except for a few dry leaves.

Jeannie's reading buddy shrugged. "It ran away from home." He screwed the lid back on the jar, placed it on the teacher's desk and wandered off.

George thought of the centipede on the bottom of his shoe and groaned.

"What's wrong?" asked Jeannie, tugging her braid.

"Nothing," said George quickly, but he was beginning to panic.

It had been an accident, but would anyone believe him? And only a creep would kill a little kid's pet. All the Mudcat kids would hate him, for sure.

George's panic increased. Maybe he'd be sent to the principal's office! Maybe they'd even call his parents from school!

George forced himself to calm down. "Nobody saw you flatten Joe the Centipede," he told himself, "so nobody has to know."

"Hi Joe," said Chad as he skipped into the room. "This apple is too long." He tossed the half-eaten apple into the garbage pail.

Choked with guilt, George remained silent.

Chad picked up the jar with a sad face. "Joe the Sen-da-peed is gone."

George felt his face grow hot. "Gone?" he croaked.

"Gone," repeated Chad.

"Oh?" George's mouth felt dry.

"He was feeling sad," Chad continued, "so he went on a trip."

"Ohhhhh?" said George. That's what they had said about George's grandfather when George was little. Instead of saying Grandpa had died, they'd said he was on a long, long trip.

But how, George wondered, could Chad know his pet was dead? Nobody had been in the room when he squashed the centipede. George held his breath and waited to see what Chad would say next.

"My sen-da-peed was happy. But now he is sad," sighed Chad.

"Well, maybe he's feeling flat," said George, thinking of the underside of his shoe. He had a sudden, horrible urge to laugh at his own sick joke. Instead he secretly gave himself a painful pinch.

"Think so?" Chad looked up at him, wide-eyed.

"Yeah, I do." Now George felt really rotten. None of this was funny. He cleared his throat. It was time to tell

Chad the truth. Well, part of the truth. But how do you explain "dead" to a four-year-old? He thought of the small wire rack at the front of their store. On its top was a sign that said "Greeting Cards for All Occasions". But this sure wasn't a greeting card occasion. Happy Birthday! Merry Christmas! Happy Hanukkah! Happy Dead Pet Day!

He'd have to just tell him. George took a deep breath. "I think Joe the Centipede is very, very gone."

Chad sat down and began to smooth the wrinkles in his socks. Then he nodded. "Joe is in the wild fron-teer. He's gone to visit King Davy Crockett. And his mommy."

Chad picked a piece of lint off his shoes and began to sing "Sleep, little sen-da-peed, sleep."

CHAPTER FIVE

It's Just Easier That Way

"Chad, since your reading buddy is here, why don't we have your Pet Show and Tell right now?" The Junior Kindergarten teacher smiled warmly at George. She was a nice, comfortable-looking lady but she was a new teacher and George could not remember her name.

Chad stopped singing his little centipede song. He brushed off the tips of his red shoes and looked up.

"No. Not today. My pet Joe has gone

away. When he comes back, I will talk about him."

"Are you sure?" The teacher looked mildly surprised.

"Yes."

"Do you know when he'll be coming back, Chad?"

Chad shook his head. "He's with King Davy. Then he's going to visit his mommy."

"That's wonderful. You let us know when he can come to school."

"All right."

"I know what a good reading buddy you have," she gave George another smile, "so I'm sure he'll want to see your pet." She looked around the room and clapped her hands. "Everybody! It's reading time!"

George felt terrible. How would he feel if someone had squashed his pet when he was four? But George couldn't remember what it was like to be four years old.

He tried to remember what his little brother had been like at that age, but it didn't help. Harold, who had always loved to get dirty, was so different from this neat-freak kid. Harold had never, ever, picked a piece of lint off his clothes.

George decided not to say anything more about Chad's pet centipede. It was just easier that way.

Chad carefully brushed off the frog pillow then sat down beside George. "Your hair is funny, Joe. Did you put it in the pencil sharpener?"

George reached up and felt his hair. It was spiky from all that tossing and turning last night. "I slept on it funny, that's all," he said gruffly. "Pick out a book and we'll read."

"You pick, Joe," said Chad.

George grabbed a picture book called *Spiders, Spiders and More Spiders*, and opened it up.

"Spiders are our friends," George read aloud. "They come in all sizes." There was a photograph of a spider-web covered in sparkling dew. Below the web dangled a huge spider.

Chad looked at the picture but then

quickly looked away. He whispered "I'm ascaired of spiders, Joe. They have long, skinny legs."

His shoulders drooped. "One night I was playing with my flashlight in the dark. But a spider dropped right down from the ceiling. Right in front of my flashlight. It made a great big shadow on the wall. All big and squiggle-lee. Then it climbed back up.

"But now I'm ascaired. Maybe the spider will drop down on my hair when I am sleeping. Maybe its long legs will crawl all over me." He touched his curls with a worried look. "So now I sleep with my head under the covers. But my cousin says only babies are ascaired of spiders. She calls me 'fraidy cat'"

George didn't mind spiders but he remembered last night's centipede nightmare. Maybe this kid wasn't so weird after all. "You know, Chad," he said, "there's nothing wrong with being afraid of spiders. Even big boys are afraid of stuff like that."

"Really, Joe?"

"Really."

"What are big boys like you afraid of?" asked Chad.

"Stuff."

Chad looked down at his shoes. "What stuff are you afraid of, Joe?"

George thought for a moment and snorted. "I'm afraid that you will never call me George."

Chad looked up and smiled. "You are funny." He pointed at the book and shook his head. "No more spiders, okay, Joe?"

That night, as George got ready for bed, he thought about Chad and his centipede. Maybe Chad could get another pet to replace Joe. Then he thought about Chad and the spider. Chad said it had dropped

42

from the ceiling right in front of the flashlight.

George knew centipedes couldn't spin silk like spiders, but he wondered if centipedes could drop down from ceilings? He nervously peered overhead, but the ceiling was bare. When he turned off the bedroom lamp, George was still thinking about centipedes and spiders and flashlights.

CHAPTER SIX

George the Genius

George woke with a jolt. Somewhere close by a siren whooped and wailed. Not again! He could hear his parents moving around in their bedroom.

Mr. Cortino appeared in the doorway carrying a flashlight and two baseball bats. He looked tired as he motioned for George to follow him down the stairs. Once again George and his dad turned off the alarm and checked out the hardware store. Nothing.

Mr. Cortino shook his head. "The alarm company guy checked the alarm out from top to bottom yesterday," he said angrily. "Didn't find a thing wrong.

Just said it's a mystery. And now," he added glumly, "everyone on Main Street is starting to complain about the noise."

There was a tap at the front door. George let Officer Silva into the shop and the two men began to talk in low voices.

George looked over at the hole where the beam of light shone across the store when the alarm system was on. He studied the shelf above it and had a sudden thought.

"Dad, let's turn off the lights, reset the alarm, and just wait for a few minutes."

"Why?" asked his dad.

"I think I know what's setting the alarm off. But I want to be sure."

Officer Silva spoke up. "Let's give the boy a chance, Juan. I can't keep coming back for all these false alarms."

"All right," Mr. Cortino said wearily. "All this getting up in the middle of the night is killing me."

After the alarm was reset, they pulled up some chairs and the three of them sat in the darkness. Silently they stared at the thin band of light that cut across the room.

"What are we looking for?" whispered Mr. Cortino.

"You'll see, Dad. Just wait."

The minutes crept by. George had to fight to keep from falling asleep. He was trying not to yawn when a slight movement just above the beam of light caught his eye. He had been right!

He nudged his dad and Officer Silva, and pointed.

The three watched as a large spider dangled above the light. As soon as it dropped down into the beam of light, the siren began to whoop and wail. The spider, frightened by the sound, clambered back up its silky thread. It quickly vanished behind the empty shelf.

"George, you're a genius!" shouted his dad. Mr. Cortino rushed to the back of the shop, flipped off the alarm, and called the good news up to the rest of the family.

"Good work, son," said Officer Silva, "you've solved the mystery." He looked over at Mr. Cortino. "I told you funny things can set these motion detectors off. Especially these older systems. Now I can get back to the rest of my beat." He got in his patrol car and drove away.

47

A few minutes later, Mrs. Cortino, who hated killing things, trapped the spider in a Kleenex then dropped it outside in the bushes. The Cortinos returned to bed in a happy mood except for Harold, who was jealous.

"Mom and Dad should have let me come downstairs all those times," Harold said bitterly, "I would have figured a spider was setting off the alarm, ages ago." Then he quickly fell asleep.

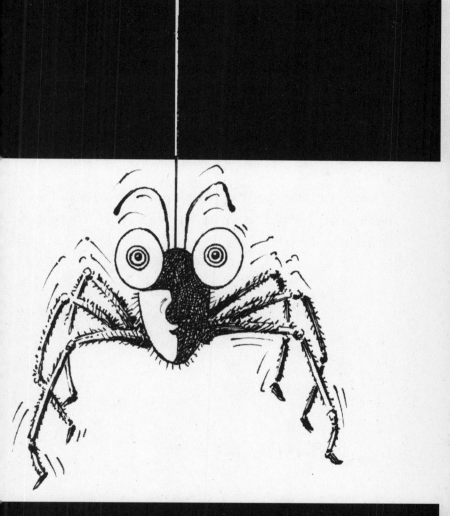

But George, too excited to sleep, lay awake in the darkness. Wait until the other Mudcat kids heard that he, not the adults, had solved the mystery. His dad had even called him a genius!

Then he remembered Joe the Centipede and his excitement faded slightly. But he still felt pretty good about himself. Surely everyone would understand. Surely everyone would agree that squashing Chad's pet had been an accident.

George thought about it some more and came to a decision. It was time to tell Chad the truth.

CHAPTER SEVEN

Spit Chips

The following Monday George brought his lunch to school, as usual. Although George lived close to J.J. Metcalf, noon was a busy time in the store for his mom and dad. Besides, it was more fun to eat with all the other Mudcat kids.

During lunch recess, a grade one kid found a worm in her sandwich. She had just taken a bite, when a tiny white worm stuck its head out of the filling. The kid burst into tears and refused to eat the rest of her sandwich. Then all the other kids in the lunch room refused to eat their sandwiches. Even George, who was not a fussy eater, had quietly tossed his out.

Too late, he discovered that Harold

had stolen his Twinkie. That pest of a brother was still jealous of George for solving the alarm mystery. George groaned. Now all he had to eat was a beat-up old banana.

George decided to fill up with water. But when he bent over to take a drink from the water fountain in the hall, he gave a snort of disgust. Although it was against the rules, kids always poured their unwanted drinks down the water fountain drain. Then the water picked up the taste of whatever had just been dumped. Chocolate milk, cola, fruit juice - George had tasted it all, coming out of that old water fountain. Today's flavor was cream of tomato soup.

"Honk! Honk! Hurry up George, I'm thirsty." Ziggy stood in line behind him, noisily munching away. With his mouth full of food he asked "Why did the cookie go to the doctor?"

"Dunno," George decided he didn't want a drink after all. But there was no escape from Ziggy's jokes.

"Because it felt crummy!"

"Ha, ha, ha," said George sourly. "Your jokes are crummy."

Ziggy looked up from a quick slurp of the funny-tasting water and spotted the school bully swaggering down the hall. "Here comes Crunch Kincaid," he muttered. "Also known as, 'If it ain't broke, break it!'" Ziggy quickly disappeared into the lunch room but George stood his ground; Crunch Kincaid only pushed smaller kids around.

"Here you go, Cortino," Crunch stuck a small bag of bar-b-que potato chips into George's hand. "I don't have time to finish these." He strolled away with a smile.

The bag was open and George could smell the mouth-watering aroma. His favorite! And he was starving!

He was about to reach inside when his brother Harold darted up, grabbed a handful of chips, and took off down the hallway. "Thanks George," he shouted back. "Mom says we have to share!" Harold crammed the chips into his mouth and disappeared around the corner.

George looked down at the bag and fumed. There were hardly any chips left.

It was time for a little 'tough love'. As the eldest, George always got blamed whenever he and Harold fought. But this time he didn't care. This time the little jerk had gone too far. Since Harold hated "wet willies" George decided he would grab the little pest and stick a wet finger in his ear.

As he stalked down the hallway after Harold, George passed Jeannie and Monica. They spotted the almost empty bag of chips in George's hand and started to laugh.

"Did Crunch give you those?" Jeannie asked.

"Yeah, why?"

"Well, don't eat 'em," said Monica, "they're 'spit chips'. We saw Crunch open the bag and spit inside."

George thought about Harold eating Crunch's spit chips and chuckled. It served the little pest right. George did-n't need to hand out any tough love today, after all.

George was still chuckling when the class set out to visit their reading buddies after lunch. Monica had given him her extra cookies so he no longer felt hungry. But then he remembered. He had to tell Chad the truth about Joe the Centipede. He squirmed at the thought.

As George walked into the JK room, Chad skipped over and tugged on his shirt. "I have a surprise for you, Joe."

"It's George."

"Come and see!" Chad led him over to a clear plastic peanut butter jar sitting on the teacher's desk. The lid, complete with air hole, was firmly in place.

"Look, there's Joe the Sen-da-peed. He's back from the wild fron-teer," said Chad.

George felt a glimmer of hope. "Really?" He peered at the jar. All he could see was a brown plastic ant lying on its back. "Is that Joe the Centipede?" he asked in amazement.

It looked a lot like the plastic ant that he had given Chad earlier. But it was brown instead of black.

"Yes! This is Joe!" Chad began to hop up and down.

"But that's not a centipede, Chad. It's an ant. A centipede has a lot more legs."

Chad took the lid off the jar and peeked inside. Then he shrugged. "Sen-da-peed is a more im-portant word."

Suddenly George felt wonderful. He hadn't squashed a little kid's pet after all! 'Joe the Centipede' was really 'Joe the Plastic Ant'.

"Do you have any gorillas in your pocket today, Joe?" Chad asked eagerly.

"Well, I do have something for you." George, now cheerful with relief, handed Chad a green plastic grasshopper.

"Thank you," Chad said eagerly. "Another friend for Joe the Sen-da-peed. Now I have two pets at school today."

He carefully slid the grasshopper into

the jar. "You are the best, Joe. Just like King Davy."

Chad smiled up at George and gently rocked the jar in his hands. Softly, he began to sing "Sleep little sen-da-peed, sleep."

THE END